L.L. Bear's
Island Adventure

Text copyright © 1992 by Kate Rowinski
Illustrations copyright © 1992 by Dawn Peterson

L.L. Bear is a trademark of L.L. Bean® Inc.
Used by permission.

ISBN 0-89272-320-3
Library of Congress Catalog Card Number 92-71972

2   4   6   8   9   7   5   3   1

Printed at J.S. McCarthy, Co., Augusta, Maine
Bound at Zahrndt's (Riverside) Bindery, Rochester, New York

DOWN EAST BOOKS   / Camden, Maine

Printed on recycled paper.

L.L. Bear's Island Adventure

By Kate Rowinski
Illustrated by Dawn Peterson

Down East Books

For weeks, the leaves had been turning from green to red and yellow and orange. It was a calm early morning, and L.L. Bear was busy packing his kayak. Today he was going to meet his friends at Blueberry Island one last time before winter.

Everything he needed fit snugly into his kayak. L.L. checked each item from his list as he packed—tent, food, red anorak, sleeping bag, spare paddle, flashlight, tide chart, and compass. It was hard to believe all his gear could fit into the little boat, but it did, and soon he was ready to go.

A sleek brown seal popped his head out of the water.

"It's a beautiful morning for a paddle!" he called.

L.L. nodded, smiling at his old friend. Simon looked so funny with his drippy, droopy whiskers that L.L. had to keep from chuckling.

Another head popped out of the water, too. It looked very much like Simon's, only smaller.

"I'd like you to meet my nephew," said Simon.

"Pleased to meet you," L.L. said to the little seal.

"Hi!" The seal pup dove under the kayak and came up on the other side. "I'm Sam, and I can do this—see?" Sam leaped out of the water and over the boat, much to L.L.'s surprise.

"That's a wonderful trick," said L.L.

"I'm big, you know." Sam pulled at his uncle's flipper. "Let's go!"

"Sam, slow down! We have all day!" Simon smiled at his nephew. "L.L., we are on our way to the island. Shall we meet you there?"

"Great!" L.L. replied. "I'm looking forward to it!"

"I'll lead, I know the way!" said Sam, diving into the water.

"Wait for me!" Simon hurried to follow his nephew. "I have so much trouble keeping up with that boy! See you later, L.L."

L.L. thought he had never seen such a pretty day. The trees on the shoreline shimmered brightly in the sun. He paddled quietly, feeling the water rush under him in gentle ripples.

All of a sudden, the quiet was shattered with an ear-splitting SQUAWK!

"Hey, old boy!" called the puffin, settling noisily onto the deck of L.L.'s kayak. "I'm glad to see you out and about today."

"Hi, Piff. It's a beautiful day. The perfect day for a picnic on the island."

"I can't wait! Last picnic of the season, don't ya know. I was about to head out to sea for the winter. But you know me—I never pass up lunch!"

Piff pointed up at the clear blue sky. "Watch the sky today," he said. "I saw storm clouds away to the west. Something's stewing, and it ain't chowder!"

"I'll be careful, Piff. Thanks." L.L. watched his friend fly away. He couldn't help thinking that Piff looked just like a wind-up toy doodlebug, flying crazily over the surface of the water.

L.L. paddled on until he saw a cloud of mist rising out of the sea. He stopped and waited, smiling to himself. Just then, a big tail rose above the surface and came down with a sharp SLAP! tumbling the little boat into the water.

L.L. popped out of the water like a cork, expertly rolling his kayak upright. His jacket was soaked, but he was laughing. "All right! What do you think you're doing? You're getting me all wet!"

L.L. came eye-to-eye with his old friend, Maddie. The whale chuckled.

"And what do you think *you're* doing, stealing a ride in the wake of a whale!" They both laughed.

"I'm glad you came today," Maddie said. "It's time for me to swim to warmer waters for the winter. I was hoping I'd get a chance to say goodbye."

"Come to Blueberry Island!" L.L. said. "Simon, Sam, Piff, and I are meeting Mackenzie Fox for a picnic."

"Oh, I'd like to see everyone!" the whale answered. "I'll meet you there!" And with a flap of her tail, she was gone.

L.L. reached Blueberry Island and pulled his boat onto the sandy beach. He got out two round honey cookies to snack on, and sat on the rocks to wait for his friends.

Mackenzie arrived first. He trotted down the shoreline, swinging a large picnic basket.

"Oh, the last picnic of the season!" sang the fox, taking out a large checkered blanket. "I'm a little worried though. My tail has been twitching all morning. I'm sure I smell rain in the air."

"It looks like you're right," L.L. said. The friendly blue sky was quickly being covered by dark, rolling storm clouds. "I hope the others get here soon."

Just as he spoke, thunder clouds roared a deep, low warning. Lightning streaked across the sky in quick, bold leaps. Raindrops began to fall, slowly at first, then more steadily, soaking the sandy beach.

"We'd better take shelter," said L.L. "Hurry!"

Mackenzie and L.L. carried everything under a rocky ledge and set out their picnic lunch. Just as they finished, Piff flew in, flapping wildly. "Maddie's here too," he said. "She's waiting for us in the cove."

"I wonder what's keeping Simon," L.L. said. "I hope he and Sam weren't caught in the storm."

Just then they saw Simon waddling quickly toward them. He looked very upset.

"Simon, what's wrong?" cried L.L., hurrying to help his friend.

"I don't know how we got separated! I've looked everywhere for him! I looked in the cove, and on that little island that only comes out at low tide, and in the seaweed gardens. But I can't find him!"

L.L., Mackenzie, and Piff looked at each other in confusion.

"Simon, what are you talking about?"

"SAM!" he said, tears coming to his eyes. "He's missing!"

The friends quickly set out to search for the missing seal pup.

"I'll check the entire island," said the fox.

"I'll search the whole bay," said the whale.

"I'll fly overhead and try to spot him," said the puffin.

"Be careful," L.L. warned the others. "The storm is still in full force."

Then he turned to Simon. "Come with me. We'll check all the coves and rocky ledges."

The wind blew fiercely, howling over their heads and sending the waves crashing over the rocks on the shoreline.

The friends searched and searched. They called Sam's name again and again. But they couldn't hear any sound above the howling wind.

"It's no use!" L.L. called to Simon. "The waves are too high. We'll have to go back and wait for the storm to die down."

Everyone met back on the beach.

"He's not on the island," said the fox. "I've checked every inch."

"He's not out in the bay," said the whale. "I even checked underwater."

"He's not anywhere on the shore," L.L. told the others.

Simon shook his head sadly. "What are we going to do?"

L.L. walked down to the water's edge. He closed his eyes and stood there for a long time, listening as hard as he could.

"Wait, do you hear that?" he called to the others. Everyone stopped talking and listened, but all they could hear was the crash of waves against the rocks.

L.L. paced up and down the beach, pausing now and then to listen. He opened his hatch and got out a big flashlight. "I'm going to look again," he said.

"But you can't!" exclaimed Piff. "Now that the wind has stopped, the fog is as thick as pea soup. You won't be able to see a thing!"

"I'll be okay," L.L. said. "I know I heard something—Sam's nearby, I'm sure of it."

L.L. strapped his flashlight onto the front of his kayak. He paddled out slowly through the deepening fog, calling Sam's name. Every now and then, he stopped to listen.

L.L. thought he heard a little whimper. "Sam?" he called. L.L. picked up the flashlight and swept the area with a beam of light. He saw nothing but a thick blanket of fog. He started to paddle on, when he heard the sound again.

"Sam?" L.L. beamed the light once more. This time, he couldn't believe his eyes.

There was Sam, clinging tightly to a large yellow bell buoy. He was crying softly.

L.L. eased the kayak up to the buoy and scooped the little seal into his big, strong arms.

"I . . . I wanted to have a race, but I made a wrong turn, and I . . . a big fish chased me—it might have been a shark, and . . . I got lost, and the fog, and . . . and my uncle . . ." he tried to explain between sobs.

"It's okay now," L.L. said softly. "Everyone's waiting for us on the island."

The animals let out a big cheer when they saw L.L. paddle up to the beach. Simon lifted Sam high into the air, hugging him tight.

"Now it's time for a real party!" he said.

L.L. smiled. "I'll say! I'm starved!"

They collected some firewood and started a fire. Then they gathered around the cheerful blaze to listen to the story of Sam's misadventure.

"Thank you for finding me," he told them. "I guess I shouldn't have gone off by myself. I'll be more careful from now on."

L.L. nodded. "It's always safer to have a buddy along on your adventures," he said. "And more fun, too!"

One by one, the animals went off to bed. L.L. set up his tent. He yawned and stretched, shivering as he looked up at the night sky. The fog had lifted, but heavy clouds still hung in the air. He gave his tent lines an extra tug to make sure they were secure. Then he crawled into his sleeping bag. It felt good to be in bed after his exciting day. In only a moment he was sound asleep.

As soon as L.L. woke, he knew something was different. The sides of his tent felt heavy and wet, and the light coming in had a strange, bright glow. He unzipped the tent flap and poked out his head.

All around him, the ground was white. Fresh snow blanketed the shoreline. Tree branches sagged heavily under the weight.

"Well, well, well." L.L. said. "Winter has decided to come, after all." He packed quickly, knowing it would be a cold trip home.

Everyone gathered to say goodbye.

It was time for Maddie to swim to warmer southern waters. "I'll see you next spring!" she called. She leaped high into the air as the friends waved goodbye, then disappeared under the surface of the dark water.

"Better be on my way too," said Piff. "I'll be back in June!" He flew off toward the open sea, where he would spend the entire winter.

Mackenzie gave the bear a big hug. "Goodbye, L.L."

"Goodbye, Mac. I'll see you in the spring."

"Come to the island when the berries are ripe. It's a treat!"

Simon and Sam left, too. "Thanks for all your help," Sam said. "We'll visit again soon." He glanced over at Simon.

". . .TOGETHER!" Everyone laughed.

L.L. paddled home in the silence of the wintry morning, gliding swiftly into the welcome shelter of his little cove. The air felt fresh and crisp. He thought it must be just about time to start waxing his skis.

L.L. stopped paddling and looked out over the ocean one last time. Autumn was gone, and with it went many of his friends.

"I'll be back soon," he called. He picked up a red maple leaf as it floated by, and let the breeze take it sailing out over the water.

"After all, Spring is just around the corner!"

And with it would come another adventure.